Chanukah A-Z

Chanukah A-Z
by Smadar Shir Sidi

illustrated by Teri Rizman Nover

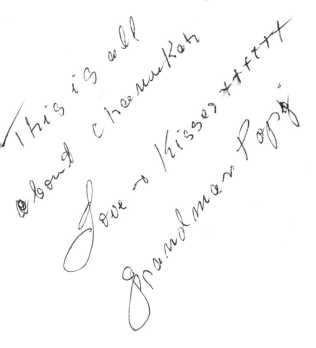

This is all
about Chanukah
Love & Kisses ++++++
grandma n Popy

Adama Books
New York

Library of Congress Cataloging-in-Publication Data

Shir, Smadar, 1957–
  Chanukah A-Z.

  Summary: Presents an anecdote, fact, or explanation relating to Chanukah
for each letter of the Hebrew alphabet.
   1. Chanukah – Juvenile literature. [1. Chanukah. 2. Hebrew language –
Alphabet. 3. Alphabet] I. Title.
BM695.H3S455   1988   296.4'35 [E]   88-16834
ISBN 1-55774-041-0

Design by Teri Nover
Printed in Israel
Adama Books, 306 West 38 Street, New York, New York 10018

To my daughters, LeeAv, Moer, Yarden

אוֹר

Or
Light

Chanukah's candles bring lots of light to the house. That is why Chanukah is also called The Festival of Lights. It is forbidden to use this holy light for reading or working, or even to kindle another candle in the menorah. Chanukah candles are only to look at, to enjoy and to publicize the miracle of Chanukah.

אֶחָד

Echad
One

Chanukah is celebrated for eight days. On the first night, the Shamash (server) is used to light one candle. Each night the number of candles is increased by one.

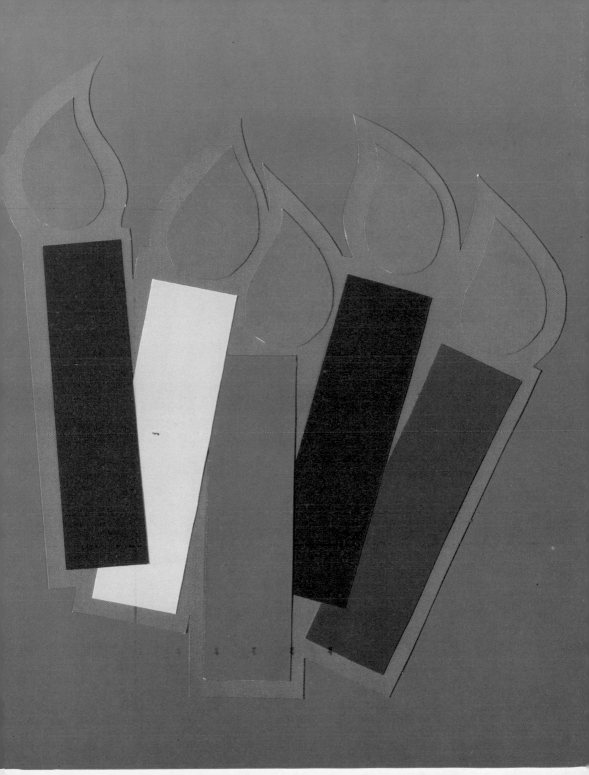

בְּרָכָה
Bracha
Blessing

Every night before kindling the Chanukah candles, we sing two blessings.

„בָּרוּךְ אַתָּה ה׳ אֱלֹהֵינוּ מֶלֶךְ הָעוֹלָם, אֲשֶׁר קִדְּשָׁנוּ בְּמִצְוֹתָיו וְצִוָּנוּ לְהַדְלִיק נֵר שֶׁל חֲנֻכָּה"

"Blessed are You, O Lord our God, King of the Universe, Who has sanctified us by Your commandments, and commanded us to kindle the lights of Chanukah."

„בָּרוּךְ . . . שֶׁעָשָׂה נִסִּים לַאֲבוֹתֵינוּ בַּיָּמִים הָהֵם בַּזְּמַן הַזֶּה"

"Bless . . . who wrought miracles for our fathers in days of old, at this season."

On the first night of Chanukah, we add the blessing Shehecheyanu:

„בָּרוּךְ . . . שֶׁהֶחֱיָנוּ וְקִיְּמָנוּ וְהִגִּיעָנוּ לַזְּמַן הַזֶּה"

"Blessed . . . Who have kept us in life and have preserved us, and enabled us to reach this period."

גִּבּוֹר

Geebor
Hero

Judah Maccabee and his soldiers were very brave. Many think that his nickname, Maccabee, is derived from the Hebrew word for hammer, in honor of his strength and his hammer – like blows to the Greeks.

דְּמֵי־חֲנֻכָּה

Dmey-Chanooka
Chanukah gelt

Gelt is the Yiddish word for money. Chanukah gelt is chocolate coins wrapped with gold foil, engraved with Chanukah symbols.

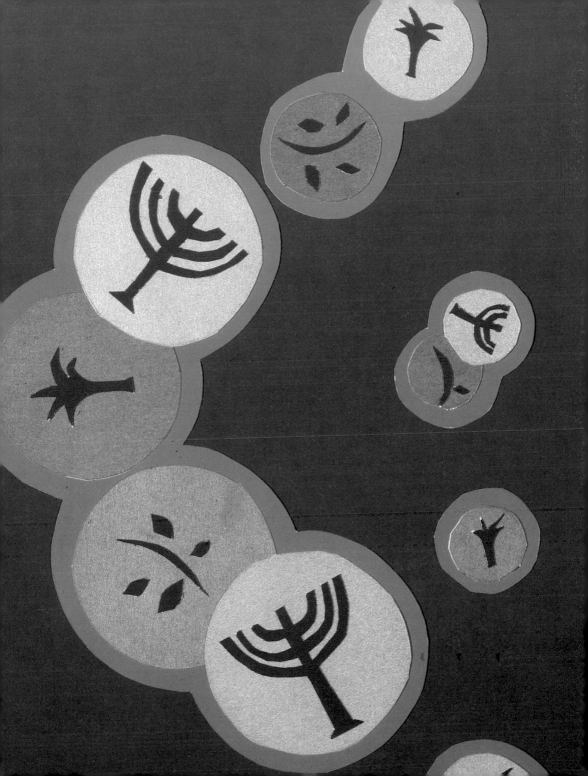

הַדְלָקָה
Hadlaka
Kindling

Each night of Chanukah the family gathers around the menorah for the ritual of saying the blessings, kindling the candles and singing Chanukah songs. The most popular Chanukah song is Rock of Ages — in Hebrew, Maoz Tzur.

וָוִים
Vaveem
Hooks

Chanukah candelabras come in all shapes and sizes and are made of metal, glass or clay. Modern versions can be hung on the wall with hooks. Many people have beautiful collections of Chanukiyot, which they remove from the walls when Chanukah arrives.

זָהָב

Zahav
Gold

One of the most precious things in the Holy Temple in Jerusalem was a large, gold menorah, a lamp with seven branches whose lights glowed continually. The Greeks broke it, but after the victory, Judah Maccabee and his soldiers repaired the menorah and lit it as part of the dedication ceremony.

חֲנֻכָּה

Chanooka
Chanukah

Chanukah is the commemoration of the Maccabee victory over the Greek army –– the few against the many. After defeating the Greeks and repairing the Temple, Judah Maccabee and his soldiers had a celebration and a dedication ceremony. In Hebrew, Chanukah means dedication ceremony.

חֲנֻכִּיָּה

Chanookeeya
Chanukiyah

A Chanukah menorah is a nine-branched candelabra lit on the eight nights of Chanukah, modeled after the Holy Temple's menorah.

טֵבֵת

Tevet
Tevet

Chanukah starts on the 25th day of the Hebrew month Kislev, the third month of the Hebrew calendar, and ends on the first week of the next month, Tevet. Chanukah is celebrated for eight days.

יְוָנִים
Yevaneem
Greeks

About two thousand years ago, the Greek king of Syria, Antiochus, took over the land of Israel and destroyed the Temple that stood in Jerusalem. He ordered the Jews to follow the Greek religion and customs and forsake their own. Although the Greek army was bigger and had better weapons, the brave Jewish army, led by Judah Maccabee, succeeded in pushing the Greeks out of Jerusalem.

יְלָדִים
Yeladeem
Children

Everyone participates in the ceremony of kindling the menorah. Many children have small ones to light next to their parents'.

כִּסְלֵו

Keeslev
Kislev

Kislev is the third month in the Hebrew calendar. Chanukah starts on the 25th of Kislev. It comes in the middle of the winter, during the month of December, and brings warmth and light to the cold days.

לְבִיבָה

Leveevah
Latke

During Chanukah it is traditional to eat foods cooked in oil as a reminder of the miracle. The most popular food is potato latkes.

לַפִּיד

Lapeed
Torch

In Israel, Chanukah is celebrated every year by a torch relay race. On the first night a torch is lit at Modi'in, a village about halfway between Tel Aviv and Jerusalem, the birthplace of the Maccabees. The torch is lit at their tombs and is relayed by runners in a race to Jerusalem, Israel's capital, where it is used to light a large menorah at the President's house.

מַכַּבִּים

Macabeem
Maccabees

Judah led the Jewish army against the Greeks. He was nicknamed Macabee. One explanation for this is that the word Maccabee was created by joining the first letters of the words in their battle cry which was displayed on their banner, "Mi Camocha Ba'elim, Adonai!" — „מִי־כָמֹךָ בָּאֵלִים, ה׳" — In English, "Who is like unto Thee, among the gods, Oh, Lord!"

נֵר

Ner
Candle

On the first night of Chanukah, the first candle is put at the far right end of the menorah (some think because Hebrew is read from right to left). Each night another candle is added to the left of the preceding candle, and the candles are lit from left to right. The candles should burn for at least half an hour, and the flames should go out by themselves.

סְבִיבוֹן

Seveevon
Dreidle

A dreidle is a four-sided top. The dreidle game reminds us of the time before the Maccabean Revolt. The Jews met secretly to study Torah and when the king's guards came by, they took stones from their pockets and pretended they were playing a game. Four Hebrew letters are engraved on the dreidle: Nun, Gimel, Hey, and Shin. They are the first letters of the Hebrew phrase, ''Nes Gadol Haya Sham,'' – – ''A great miracle happened there.'' On Israeli dreidles, the letter Shin is changed to Peh – – ''a great miracle happened here.''

סוּפְגָּנִיָּה

Soofganeeyah
Sufganiyah

Sufganiyot are Israeli doughnuts eaten during Chanukah. They are fried in hot oil in remembrance of the miracle of the cruse of oil.

עֶרֶב

Erev
Evening

The Chanukah candles are lit in the evening after sunset, when it's late enough for them to bring light and draw attention, but early enough for everyone in the family, including young children, to enjoy the ceremony. On Friday night, the lighting of the menorah precedes the lighting of the Shabbat candles. On Saturday night the menorah is lit after the Havdalah.

פַּך

Pach
Cruse

To celebrate the victory over the Greeks and the dedication of the Temple, the Maccabees wanted to light the menorah. They looked everywhere for oil, but found none until they discovered one small cruse of oil. It contained only enough oil to last for one day, but a miracle happened – the oil lasted for eight days, giving them enough time to prepare new oil to keep the menorah lit.

צֶבַע
Tzevah
Color

Chanukah is colorful. The menorah candles come in a variety of colors:

אָדוֹם	צָהוֹב	כָּחוֹל	יָרוֹק	לָבָן
Adom	Tzahov	Cachol	Yarok	Lavan
Red	Yellow	Blue	Green	White

קָנִים
Kaneem
Branches of candelabra

A Chanukah menorah has nine branches, so that the candles are separated from one another and the flames do not look like one.

רְחוֹב
Rechov
Street

It is customary to place the menorah near a window facing the street to proclaim the miracle. That way people who don't celebrate Chanukah see the candles and know what night of Chanukah it is.

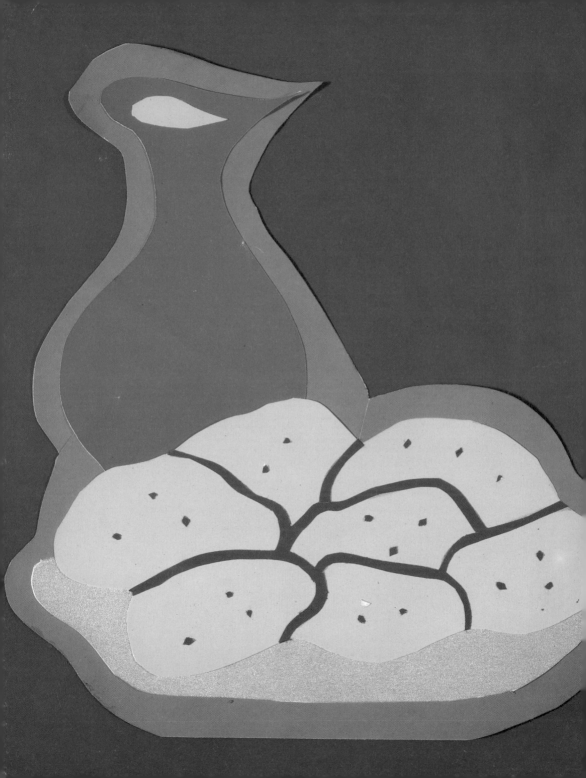

שֶׁמֶן

Shemen
Oil

In the days of the Temple, the menorah was lit with pure olive oil kept in containers sealed by the high priest. After defeating the Greeks, only one cruse of oil was found, but miraculously its contents lasted for eight days.

שַׁמָּשׁ

Shamash
Server

The Shamash is separated from the other branches of the menorah. Shamash, in Hebrew, "server," is used to kindle the other candles.

תַּפּוּחַ־אֲדָמָה

Tapooach- Adamah
Potato

The latke is the most popular Chanukah food. Made from potatoes with some onion, eggs and flour, it is fried in oil, and served with apple sauce.